Color The Rainforest

About Mothers & Others for a Livable Planet

Mothers & Others works nationally to call attention to environmental issues affecting children and families; to empower families to work for solutions to environmental problems; and to press for federal, state, and local policies that will ensure a healthy and livable planet. Mothers & Others for a Livable Planet is a project of NRDC. Membership in Mothers & Others is $15. For more information, write: Mothers & Others, 40 West 20th Street, New York, NY 10011

About the Natural Resources Defense Council (NRDC)

NRDC is one of the nation's premier environmental protection organizations. Now celebrating its 20th anniversary, NRDC is backed by 160,000 members and has a staff of over 80 lawyers, scientists, and environmental specialists working in five offices nationwide. NRDC led the successful citizen fights against lead in gasoline, CFCs in aerosols, and Alar in apples. NRDC is launching a major public education campaign in 1990 to help save rainforests worldwide as well as our nation's own unique and vanishing tropical forests in Hawaii, Puerto Rico, the U.S. Virgin Islands, and American Samoa.

Published in the United States by Living Planet Press, 558 Rose Avenue, Venice, CA 90291

Written by: Dwight Holing
Cover design: William Whitehead
Typography: Berna Alvarado-Rodriguez
Inside illustrations: Carol Benioff

Printed on recycled paper

**To order more copies of this book, please see last page.
Discounts are available for bulk orders.**

INTRODUCTION

Picture a land where monkeys swing in trees, where flowers grow so big that frogs can swim inside them after a rainstorm, and where more kinds of plants and animals live than there are names to go around. Picture the rainforest.

Tropical rainforests grow in a band that circles the middle of the Earth like a belt around your waist. They are drenched by rain and dazzled by sunshine. This makes the air as warm and moist as the inside of a greenhouse—perfect for plants to grow in. And anywhere there is plenty of vegetation, there is sure to be plenty of insects, birds, and animals.

Rainforests are very special places. They provide a home for many unusual creatures. In South America, flocks of parrots chatter in the treetops. In Asia, pygmy hippopotamuses wallow in the rivers. In Hawaii, honeycreepers sip nectar from bright red flowers. And in Africa, gorillas munch on leaves.

People also live in the rainforest. Tribes of native people live in villages just as they have for thousands of years—long before cars and televisions were invented.

Rainforests give us lots of food and other useful things. Bananas come from the rainforest. So do sugar and cinnamon. The sap from rubber trees gives balls their bounce, rubber bands their snap. Other plants and flowers from the rainforest are used to make medicine to make us well when we are sick. Rainforest trees also help control our weather, clean our air, and prevent floods.

Because rainforests give us so much, it is important that we protect them. You can help by learning all you can about the rainforest and the remarkable plants, animals, and people that live there.

So color the rainforest. Color it green. More plants and trees grow there than anywhere else. Color it black and brown. All kinds of native people live in the rainforest. Color it red, blue, yellow, and every shade in between. The birds and flowers of the rainforest come in every color of the rainbow. But most of all, color the rainforest wonderful. There is no place like it on Earth!

Big cats are the kings of the rainforest. In Central and South America, the jaguar reigns, while leopards stalk the forest of Java and tigers prowl India.

Yellow as a banana
and just as big, the bill
of the toucan allows
this tropical bird to
crunch seeds and fruits
with ease.

The blossom of the rosy periwinkle may be tiny, but it is big in the world of medicine. Doctors use the drug made from this rainforest beauty to help make people well when they are sick.

Everything gets decorated, even the people, when the Kayapo of Brazil's Amazon Basin hold a ceremony. Women adorn their hair with beads and feathers and color their entire bodies with bright paints.

Velvety gray anteaters
use long, powerful
claws to root out insects
and even longer tongues
that are as sticky as tape
to lap them up.

Their skin patterned like leaves, pythons can grow as long as a garden hose and as big around as a tree limb— big enough to swallow a pig in one bite.

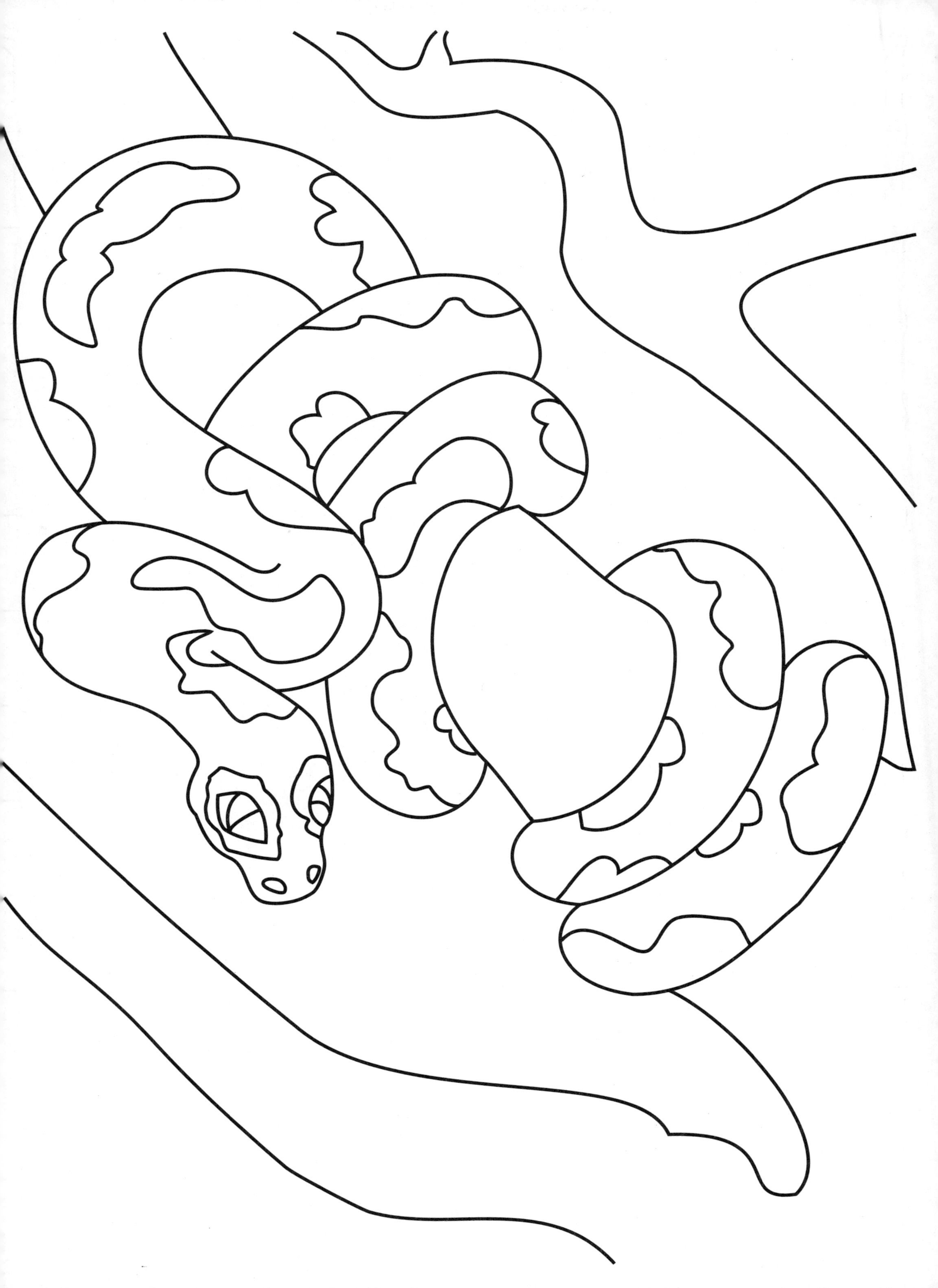

The plants and animals of the rainforest provide the Penan people of Borneo with everything they need. Women weave beautiful mats and baskets from the fiber of plants.

The quetzal is the royal bird of Central America. Its head is crowned with gold feathers and its long, flowing tail feathers trail behind like a scarlet cape.

Some bromeliads are called "pitcher plants." And for good reason. When it rains, they hold water. No wonder frogs like to live inside their petals.

Though you might mistake them for raccoons, ring-tailed lemurs actually are primates, closely related to monkeys.

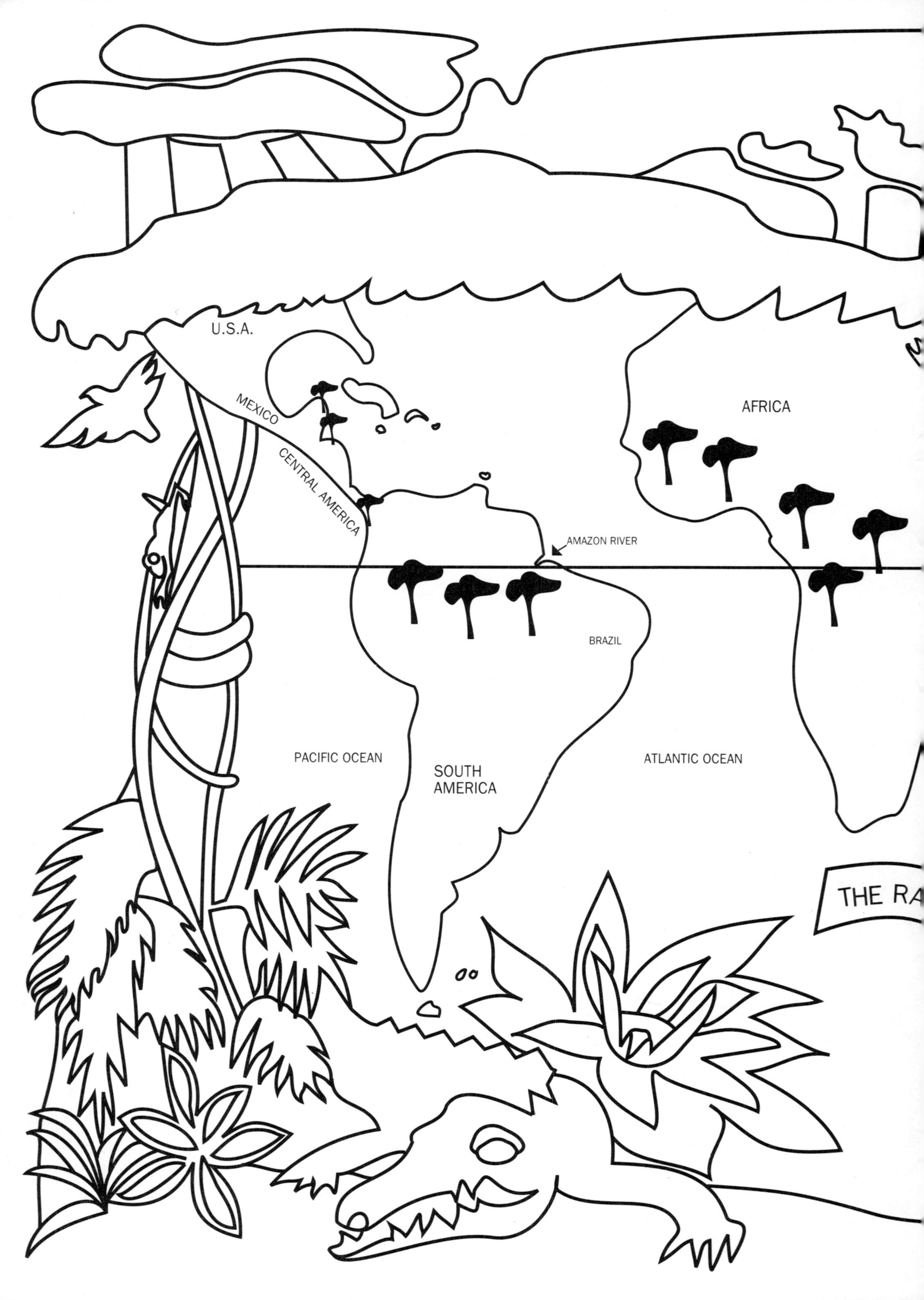
U.S.A.
MEXICO
CENTRAL AMERICA
AFRICA
AMAZON RIVER
BRAZIL
PACIFIC OCEAN
SOUTH
AMERICA
ATLANTIC OCEAN
THE RA

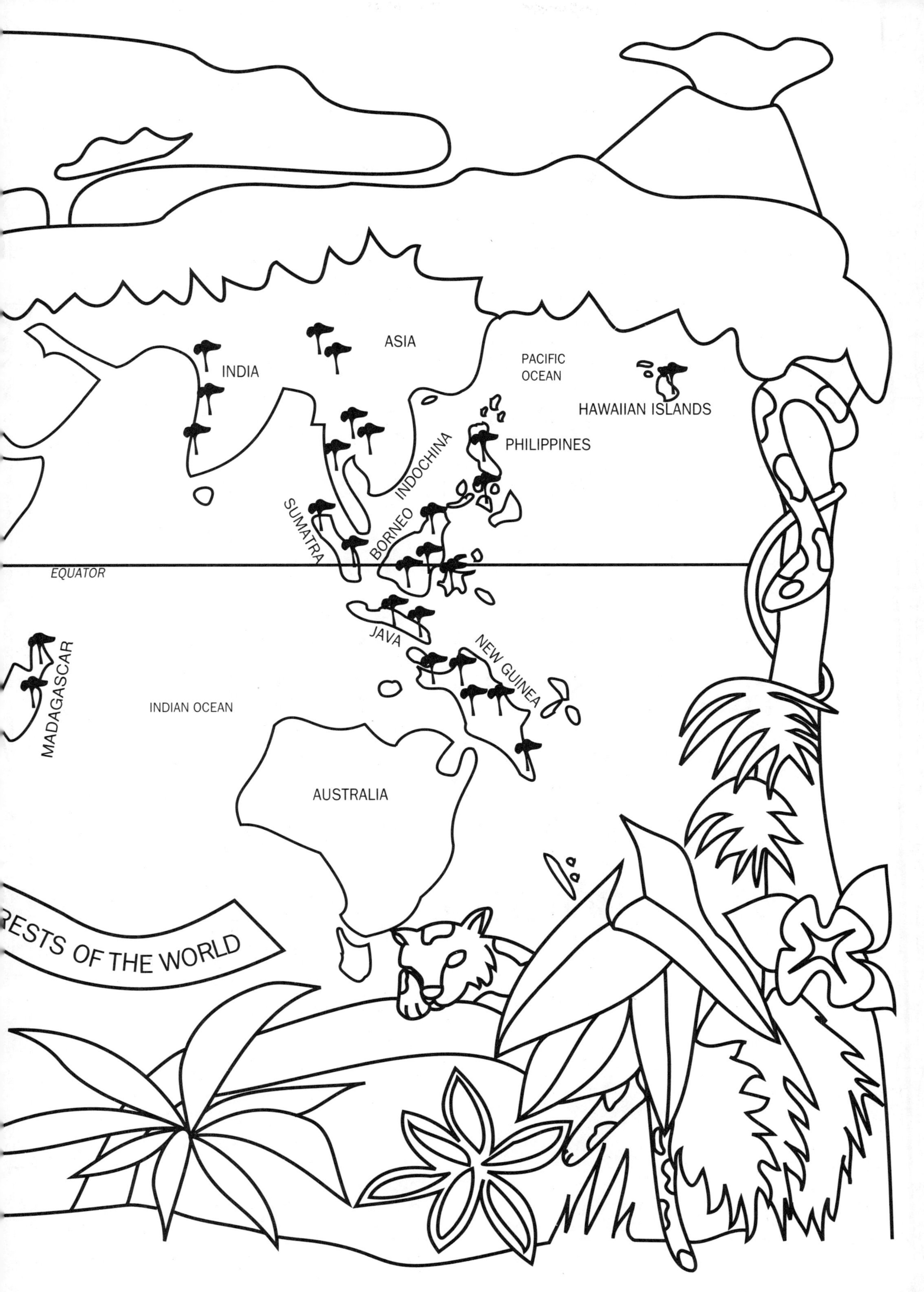
ASIA
INDIA
PACIFIC
OCEAN
HAWAIIAN ISLANDS
PHILIPPINES
INDOCHINA
SUMATRA
BORNEO
EQUATOR
JAVA
NEW GUINEA
MADAGASCAR
INDIAN OCEAN
AUSTRALIA
RESTS OF THE WORLD

Their faces become a living stage when the Huli tribe of Papua New Guinea perform their ritual "sing sings." The men paint themselves yellow and red and wear enormous hats capped with multicolored feathers.

Like a tapestry
unfurled, the wings of
the atlas moth of Java
are a rich texture
of browns and yellows.

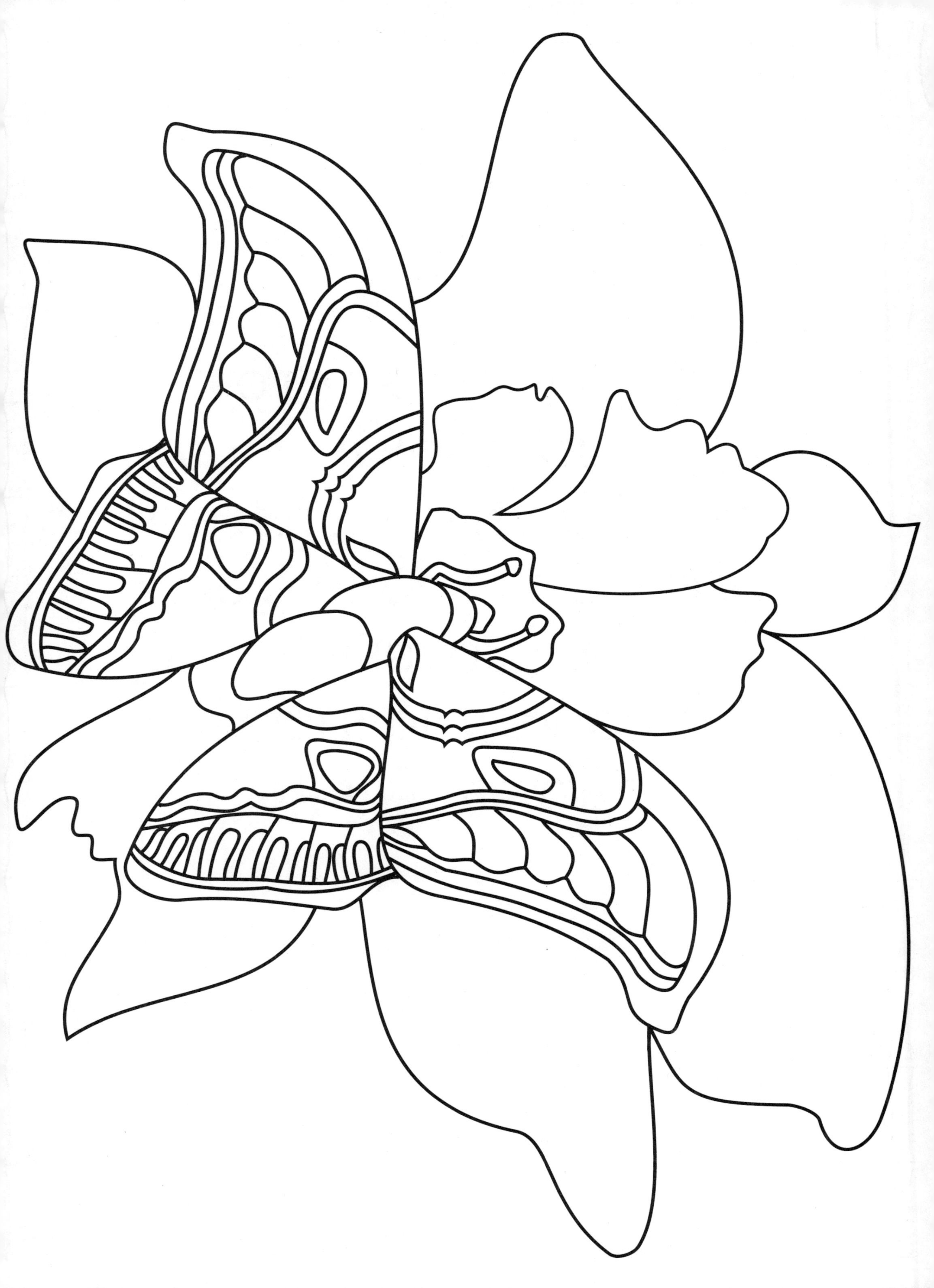

The Efe never grow taller than four or five feet. But these African pygmies are courageous hunters. Boys learn to use bows and arrows at an early age.

What animal has "five hands"? It is the muriqui of Brazil. This spider monkey uses its tail to help it climb and hang from trees.

Brazilian rubber tappers are careful not to hurt the trees when they take sap from their trunks. Rubber tree sap, called latex, is used to make everything from rubber balls to car tires.

The United States has tropical rainforests of its own. In Hawaii, beautiful flowers like the hibiscus cover the mountainsides.

A yellow sun
surrounded by a
rainbow of red flowers
lights up the mask of
the Gimi, a tribe of
people who live in the
rainforests of
Papua New Guinea.

When flocks of macaws fly overhead, the sky becomes a moving rainbow. These large parrots come in all colors—scarlet, blue, green, and yellow.

Brown howlers
are aptly named.
These elflike monkeys
roar as loudly
as a lion.

The bird-of-paradise
grows in many of our
gardens, but this blue
and orange flower
is actually a native of
tropical lands.

Slower than molasses,
baby three-toed sloths
cling to their mothers
until they are old
enough to climb trees
on their own.

Rainforest Rescue Products

All proceeds from these NRDC sales go to rainforest preservation and other programs in defense of threatened environments.

The Rainforest Book—How You Can Save the World's Rainforests

The Rainforest Book is every person's window into the spectacular world of tropical rainforests—their amazing diversity, the threats to their survival, and the ways we can preserve them for future generations. This easy-to-read handbook is full of practical tips for turning your concern for rainforests into action.
112 pages; $5.95; **Item #101**

Color the Rainforest

The perfect educational gift for children ages 3–7.
48 pages; $4.95; **Item #102**

Amazon Days, Amazon Nights—an audio adventure

Enter the mysterious world of the Amazon jungle through this beautiful hi-fidelity audiotape. Produced on location by one of the world's premier nature recordists, NRDC's Special Edition of *Amazon Days, Amazon Nights* captures the living symphony of the rainforest as you've never heard it before. Great for all ages.
40 minute cassette; $7.95; **Item #103**

Rescue the Rainforest T-Shirt

Wear the brilliant hues of the rainforest with this beautiful T-shirt. 100% premium cotton.
Adult Size: $14.95; **Item #104**
Child Size: $12.95; **Item #105**

• Cut along dotted line, or photocopy form, fill out and mail along with your check to NRDC, P.O. Box 1400, Church Hill, MD 21690 •

ORDERING INSTRUCTIONS

- Please make your check or money order payable to NRDC
- Send to: NRDC, P.O. Box 1400, Church Hill, MD 21690

Name: ____________________

Address: ____________________

____

- Please add $2.00 for shipping
- Your donation of $15 or more will enroll you in NRDC's **Mothers & Others for a Livable Planet**—which entitles you to a full year's subscription to **tlc** ("*truly* loving care for our kids and our planet").

QTY.	ITEM #	UNIT PRICE	TOTAL
	106	DONATION	$
		SHIPPING	$ 2.00
		TOTAL	$